PEDRO

PEDRO GOES BUGGY

by Fran Manushkin

illustrated by Tammie Lyon

PICTURE WINDOW BOOKS
a capstone imprint

Pedro is published by Picture Window Books,
a Capstone Imprint
1710 Roe Crest Drive
North Mankato, Minnesota 56003
www.mycapstone.com

Text © 2017 Fran Manushkin
Illustrations © 2017 Picture Window Books

Library of Congress Cataloging-in-Publication Data
Names: Manushkin, Fran, author. | Lyon, Tammie, illustrator.
Title: Pedro goes buggy / by Fran Manushkin ; [illustrator, Tammie Lyon].
Description: North Mankato, Minnesota : Picture Window Books, an imprint of
    Capstone Press, [2017] | Series: Pedro | Summary: Pedro collects a
    lot of different bugs for a class assignment, but when his brother lets
    them out in the house their parents are furious, and ban any further
    collecting.
Identifiers: LCCN 2015046881| ISBN 9781515800859 (library binding) | ISBN
    9781515800897 (pbk.) | ISBN 9781515800934 (ebook (pdf))
Subjects: LCSH: Hispanic Americans—Juvenile fiction. | Brothers—Juvenile fiction.
    | Insects—Juvenile fiction. | Science projects—Juvenile fiction. | CYAC: Hispanic
    Americans—Fiction. | Brothers—Fiction. | Insects—Fiction. | Science projects—
    Fiction.
Classification: LCC PZ7.M3195 Pc 2017 | DDC 813.54—dc23
LC record available at http://lccn.loc.gov/2015046881

Designer: Aruna Rangarajan and Tracy McCabe

Design Elements: Shutterstock

Photo Credits:
Greg Holch, pg. 26
Tammie Lyon, pg. 26

Printed and bound in the USA.
102016   010083R

Table of Contents

Chapter 1
Wild About Bugs

"Who likes bugs?" asked

Miss Winkle.

"I do!" yelled Pedro. "I am

wild about bugs!"

"Me too," said Katie Woo. "I like the green bugs that are called katydids."

"Ha!" Pedro smiled. "You would!"

"We are going to study bugs," said Miss Winkle. "After school, go out and look for bugs. Pick one that you like and write about it."

"I like stinkbugs!" shouted

Roddy. "I can bring one to

school. That would be fun!"

   "Not a good

idea," said

Miss Winkle.

Pedro went home and
found his bug jar.

He began looking for bugs
in the weeds. He found ten
ants and put them in his jar.

Pedro told JoJo, "Flies are
fun too. But they are hard to
catch."

"Not for my cat," bragged
JoJo.

"Spiders are cool," Pedro
told his mother. "I'll bring
some home."

"No way!" said his mom.
"Ants are fine, but no spiders!"

Pedro found a field with lots of ladybugs. He took home fifteen. His puppy, Peppy, tried to eat them.

"No way!" yelled Pedro.

Pedro loved

beetles too.

"They are so

shiny," he told JoJo.

"And they are fun to say," he

added. "Beetle, beetle, beetle!"

He took home twenty.

Chapter 2
Bed Bugs, Head Bugs

Pedro couldn't stop

catching bugs! Each day he

found more.

He told his little brother,

Paco, "It's a good thing I have

a big jar!"

One day, when Pedro was at school, Paco told the bugs, "I want to watch you run around."

He opened the jar and let them out!

There were bugs on the bed

and bugs on Paco's head.

"Cool!" he said.

When Pedro came home,

he said, "Not cool!"

"Out they go!" said Pedro's dad. "These bugs are driving me buggy."

Chapter 3
Get Hopping

The next day, Pedro told

Katie, "I have no bugs to write

about."

"You better hurry and

find one," said Katie. "Get

hopping."

"I love hopping!" said

Pedro. He hopped down the

block looking for a new bug.

He saw a wasp. "No way!"

he yelled.

He saw a grasshopper

jumping in the weeds.

"Let's race!" Pedro yelled.

Pedro hopped. Then the grasshopper jumped.

"It's a tie!" yelled JoJo. "You both win!"

Pedro told the grasshopper,

"You are the most fun. I will

write about you."

Pedro wrote about the

grasshopper. Then he let

him go.

"Good work," said Miss Winkle. "Next we will be writing about tigers."

"Great!" Pedro smiled. "I can't wait to bring one home."

About the Author

Fran Manushkin is the author
of many popular picture books,
including *Happy in Our Skin*; *Baby,
Come Out!*; *Latkes and Applesauce:
A Hanukkah Story*; *The Tushy
Book*; *The Belly Book*; and *Big Girl
Panties*. Fran writes on her beloved
Mac computer in New York City, without the
help of her two naughty cats, Chaim and Goldy.

About the Illustrator

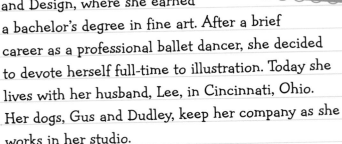

Tammie Lyon began her love for
drawing at a young age while
sitting at the kitchen table with
her dad. She continued her love
of art and eventually attended
the Columbus College of Art
and Design, where she earned
a bachelor's degree in fine art. After a brief
career as a professional ballet dancer, she decided
to devote herself full-time to illustration. Today she
lives with her husband, Lee, in Cincinnati, Ohio.
Her dogs, Gus and Dudley, keep her company as she
works in her studio.

Glossary

bragged (BRAGD)—talked about how good you are at something

katydid (KAY-tee-did)—a large, green bug that is like a grasshopper

shiny (SHY-nee)—very smooth and bright

wasp (WOSP)—a flying bug that has a thin body; female wasps can give a painful sting

wild (WILDE)—going beyond what is usual

Let's Talk

1. Pedro loves all kinds of bugs. What's your favorite type of bug? Why do you like it?

2. Miss Winkle tells the kids to go out and look for bugs to write about. Where does Pedro find bugs? Where would you go to look for bugs?

3. Pedro's mom does not like spiders. How do we know that? Which bugs don't you like?

Let's Write

1. Pedro writes about a grasshopper. Write down three facts about your favorite bug. If you can't think of three, ask a grown-up to help you find some in a book or on the computer.

2. Draw a picture of what your favorite bug looks like. Then write a short story about it.

3. Think about all the different types of bugs that Pedro caught in his jar. Write them down in a list. Then write the names of all the other types of bugs you can think of.

JOKE AROUND

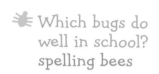

🐝 Which bugs do
well in school?
spelling bees

🐝 Name the fastest bug in the world.
the quicket

🐝 Which insects are knows for their
good manners?
ladybugs

🐝 What is the biggest ant in the world?
an elephant

🐝 What do spiders like with their
hamburgers?
French flies

🦗 What is a bee's favorite treat?
bumble gum

🦗 How do bees get to work?
They take the buzz.

🦗 Which bugs are the messiest?
litterbugs

🦗 What kind of music do
grasshoppers like?
hip-hop

THE FUN DOESN'T STOP HERE!

Discover more at www.capstonekids.com

- 🐜 Videos & Contests
- 🐜 Games & Puzzles
- 🐜 Friends & Favorites
- 🐜 Authors & Illustrators

Find cool websites and more books like this one at www.facthound.com. Just type in the Book ID: 9781515800859 and you're ready to go!